THIS BOOK BELONGS TO :

SBN 361 00424 9

Published by Purnell Books, Paulton, Bristol,
BS18 5LQ, a member of the BPCC group of companies.
Reprinted 1983
Made and printed in Great Britain by Purnell and Sons
(Book Production) Ltd, Paulton, Bristol.

NODDY
AND THE AEROPLANE

BY

Enid Blyton

CONTENTS

1. Noddy Gives Tubby a Job
2. Tubby Bear Works Very Hard
3. Whatever is Wrong with the Car?
4. Oh, You Bad Little Tubby Bear!
5. A Wonderful Surprise for Noddy!
6. Noddy Learns to Fly
7. Tubby is Rather Silly
8. Noddy and the Aeroplane

LONDON
SAMPSON LOW, MARSTON & CO., LTD.
AND RICHARDS PRESS LTD.

© Enid Blyton
as to the text herein and
Sampson Low, Marston & Co. Ltd.
as to the artwork herein 1963

"AN AEROPLANE I CAN DRIVE MYSELF!"
CRIED NODDY

6

1. NODDY GIVES TUBBY A JOB

ONE day Noddy came home quite tired out. He really had had a very busy day!

"I feel too tired even to give you a clean, little car," he said. "And you're very *very* dirty, because it's such muddy weather."

"Parp-parp," said the car, in a very little voice. It didn't like being *quite* so dirty.

"I feel too tired even to sing a song," said Noddy, getting out of the car. "And I *had* thought of a very nice little coming-home song. It began like this, car: 'How nice it is to be home for tea, in a dear little house that is fond of me, and a . . .'"

"Noddy! Hallo, Noddy!" called a voice over the fence. "Did you have a good day? Ooooh, isn't your car dirty!"

"Oh, hallo, little Tubby Bear," said Noddy, shutting his garage door. "How many spankings have *you* had today? I hear you've been very

very naughty lately. It's just about time you did something good for a change."

"I'd like to, Noddy," said Tubby, climbing over the fence. "I'd like to very much. Are you tired? Can I do something for *you*? I really *do* want to be good. I'm tired of being naughty."

"You're tired of getting spankings, you mean," said Noddy. "Now, if I could only *trust* you to be good, I'd ask you to clean my dirty little car. I really feel too tired to get out my pail and my cloths, and . . ."

"NODDY! I'll clean your car all over, I'll make it shine and gleam, I'll make it as good as new!" shouted Tubby, in excitement. "Oh, LET me clean it! I can pretend it

is *my* car. I'll get every speck of dirt off it, I'll . . ."

"All right, all right, don't shout," said Noddy, putting his hands over his ears. "You *could* clean my car well, I'm sure, but I just don't trust you. You'd do something silly—take the hooter off and not be able to put it on again—or even take the wheels off to clean, and let them roll away down the road. I know you, Tubby. You may be small but you can make Very Big Mistakes."

"Please, PLEASE, dear Noddy, let me clean your car," begged Tubby. "You're always telling me to be good, and so are my father and mother, and now, when I want to be, you won't let me."

"Oh well—*clean* the car then," said Noddy. "I'm too tired to stand here talking to you. There are the cloths, look—and remember you've got to wash them out when you've finished with them, and hang them out to dry on my line. And remember to put the lid on the polish tin—and don't DARE to try and drive the car, or I'll—I'll— well, I really don't know *what* I'd do to you. Throw you into the pond, I think."

"Oh, *Noddy*! Thank you, thank you for saying I can clean the car!" said little Tubby Bear, so joyful that he just had to fling his arms round Noddy. Down

9

went Noddy on the ground with a bump!

And at the very same moment who should come in at the gate but the Bumpy-Dog, leaping up and down as usual, and barking in delight to see Noddy on the ground. He thought that Noddy and Tubby were having a game, and he flung himself on poor Noddy and licked him all over his face.

"Bumpy-Dog! STOP it!" shouted Noddy.

"When I want my face washed, I'll wash it myself. Pull him off me, Tubby Bear, and don't stand there laughing!"

"Bumpy! Come away from Noddy!" shouted Tubby. "Bumpy, you can help me to clean Noddy's car. BUMPY!"

Bumpy left Noddy and ran over to Tubby at once. Clean Noddy's car! What a very grand thing to do! He leapt happily up to lick Tubby's face, and down went Tubby, of course. Noddy got up and went indoors. Let Bumpy knock down Tubby Bear, let them both clean his car, let Tubby polish *Bumpy* if he wanted to instead of the car—all

Noddy wanted was a nice hot cup of tea and a sit-down.

Tessie Bear, who was just passing by, saw him going slowly indoors, looking half asleep. She called to him, "You look tired, Noddy. I'll come and make tea for you. I've a ginger cake here. We'll have a nice tea together. Would you like that?"

"Oh *yes*, Tessie Bear!" said Noddy, pleased. "I feel just like eating a ginger cake. Oh, Tessie, I *am* pleased to see you. I feel very fond of bears just at the moment. There's Tubby in my garage cleaning my dirty car for me—and you coming to tea—with a ginger cake, too!"

"I'm surprised that you let that naughty little Tubby Bear clean your car," said Tessie. "He might easily drive it away!"

"He can't," said Noddy. "The petrol tank is empty. Oh, Tessie, let's have tea quickly. I'm so hungry."

And soon he and little Tessie Bear were sitting down by the fire, eating toast made by

Noddy, and drinking tea made by Tessie, and enjoying the lovely ginger cake. But it wasn't peaceful for very long! Someone came and flung himself against the front door, and made Noddy jump so much that he spilt his tea.

"Woof!" said a voice.

"That's the Bumpy-Dog!" said Tessie. "I locked him up. However did he get out? Bumpy-Dog, go home!"

> "Go home, Bumpy-Dog,
> We're having our tea,
> So please don't disturb
> Little Tessie and me!"

yelled Noddy.

But the Bumpy-Dog joined them just the same! He suddenly leapt in through the open window, and jumped up at Noddy, making him drop his toast. "Oh, BUMPY! Go away! Look at my nice toast—butter-side down, too. GO AWAY!"

2. TUBBY BEAR WORKS VERY HARD

THE Bumpy-Dog wouldn't go away, even when Tessie smacked him. He put himself into a corner, and whined tiny little whines, so that Noddy soon felt very sorry for him. Then suddenly he leapt up and barked so loudly that he quite scared Tessie and Noddy. He ran to the door, he growled, he pawed at the bottom of the door, and even threw himself at it till the door shook from top to bottom.

Noddy and Tessie were very surprised. "There must be someone outside—a burglar perhaps," said Tessie, in a scared little voice.

"HO! I'M not scared of burglars!" said Noddy, bravely, and he went to the door and flung it open. It was only little Tubby Bear! He had seen Tessie going into Noddy's house with the ginger cake on a dish, and it had made him feel very hungry for his tea!

"Please, Noddy, I've finished cleaning your car, and it looks very nice. I thought you'd like to come and see it," said Tubby. "Oooooh! What a LOVELY ginger cake!"

"You'd better share it, as you're being kind enough to clean Noddy's car," said Tessie Bear, kindly. "Come in."

"Wait a minute," said Noddy. "I'd rather like to go and see if Tubby *has* cleaned my car well before we waste any ginger cake on him. It might be only half-done."

So out they went to look at the little car. My goodness me, Tubby had certainly worked hard! The little car shone and gleamed and glinted like new.

"Oh, TUBBY!" said Tessie Bear, surprised. "It really DOES look lovely! How hard you must have worked! You certainly MUST come and have some ginger cake!"

Little Tubby was very pleased. He was so hungry that he ate three huge slices, and Tessie had to stop him. "Just *look* at your tummy!" she said. "You'll burst in a minute. No more cake, Tubby."

"I don't want any re-ward for cleaning your

"YOU LOOK AS GOOD AS NEW, LITTLE CAR,"
SAID NODDY

car, Noddy," said Tubby, undoing his belt a little. "But I would just like *one* thing."

"What's that?" asked Noddy.

"Let me drive it down the road and back," said Tubby.

"NO," said Noddy. "Anyway, it hasn't any petrol in the tank. NO, Tubby. I'm very grateful to you for cleaning my car so well and I'll give you a free ride whenever I see you—but you are NOT going to drive my car—no, not even push it out of the garage and let it run down the hill! You'd probably knock half a dozen lamp-posts over, and Mr. Plod would be after me at once."

"All right," said Tubby, sadly. "But couldn't

you make up a little song about me? I'd like that so much."

"Oh, all right, Tubby," said Noddy. "Eat your fourth slice of cake, and I'll sing a song about you."

So while Tubby ate his fourth slice of cake Noddy sang this little song:

"Oh, Tubby Bear, how good you are
  To go and clean my little car,
  You rubbed with all your might and main
  To make it nice and clean again.
  So dear kind Tubby Bear, please take
  What's left of Tessie's ginger cake,
  And eat it all, it won't last long . . .
  And that's the finish of my song!"

"Oh, that's lovely, Noddy," said Tubby in delight. "I wish I could make up songs like you. How do you do it?"

"I don't know," said Noddy. "They just come into my head and I sing them. Well—you take the rest of the cake, and go now. I DO think you have cleaned my car well."

Tubby Bear went off with the cake, looking very proud and pleased. What *would* Mr. and Mrs. Tubby Bear, his father and mother, say, when he told them how clever he had been?

Tessie Bear washed up the tea-things, and then Noddy said he would take her home in the car. But she shook her head.

"No thank you, Noddy. The Bumpy-Dog hasn't had a proper run today. I'll walk home with him."

When he heard the word "walk" the Bumpy-Dog went quite mad, and leapt right over the tea-table. Tessie was really shocked at him.

"What *bad* manners, Bumpy!" she said. "I shan't take you out to tea again."

That made Bumpy put his tail down at once, and he went to sit all by himself in a corner. "It's all right, Bumpy," said Noddy, patting him. "You didn't knock the teapot over, though your tail only *just* missed it! Take Tessie Bear home now, and guard her well."

That made Bumpy feel much better, and his tail began to wag again. He went off with Tessie Bear, walking proudly in front of her, growling at any car that passed. Woof! Grrrrr! Don't you dare to splash Tessie Bear, cars!

Noddy went to his garage to look at his little car again, shining so very brightly.

"You look as good as new!" he said. "You do really! I'm sure Big-Ears will think I've bought a new car when he sees you. Oh—there *is* Big-Ears! Hey, Big-Ears, have you come to see me? Well, just look at my car!"

"Good gracious—is it *really* your car, Noddy?" said Big-Ears, surprised. "I've never seen it looking so bright and so clean. Did *you* clean it?"

"No—that naughty little Tubby Bear did it for me," said Noddy, nodding his head up and down. "You wouldn't think such a bad little fellow could clean a car so well, would you? Won't everyone stare when I take it out to-morrow!"

"My word, yes!" said Big-Ears. "Come and call for me, Noddy, and we'll go and have an ice-cream together. I'd feel proud to ride in a car as smart as yours is now! So don't forget —call for me tomorrow!"

Well, wasn't that nice of Big-Ears? You'll have a good time tomorrow, Noddy!

3. WHATEVER IS WRONG WITH
THE CAR?

NOW the next morning, when Noddy had washed up his breakfast things, and polished the bell on his hat, and made his bed, and put a little pie into the oven, he went to the garage to get out his car. He sang all the time.

"It's time for shopping, little car,
  Goodness me, how clean you are!
  Everyone will shout and say,
  LOOK AT NODDY'S CAR TODAY!"

"First of all, little car, I'll let you run down the hill to the garage, and have some petrol put into your tank," he said. "It must be quite empty after that long run you and I went the other day. Come along!"

He hopped into the car and pressed the starter, expecting to hear the car's usual happy noise. But instead of that it made a very curious sound indeed.

"Eekoff! Eekoff! Eekoff!"

And then it began to shake every time it said "Eekoff", and Noddy bounced up and down as it shook.

"Car! Little car! What's wrong with you?" cried Noddy. "You keep jerking and jumping! You just stand here and jerk. What's happened?"

Noddy got out and looked under the car. It seemed all right. Then he tried it again. No—it just went "eekoff, eekoff" and jerked again. Noddy sat down on a sack in the garage and wailed.

"Something's wrong with my car! It says Eekoff all the time, and it won't go. Oh, *why* did I let Tubby Bear clean it for me yesterday? Why did I? Something's gone wrong with you, little car. Wait till I get hold of Tubby Bear—I'll shake him till all the buttons fly off his coat!"

"Eekoff," said the little car, mournfully, and jerked up and down again.

Noddy ran into the garden and yelled at the top of his voice. "Tubby! Tubby! Where are you, you wicked little bear? What have you done to my car? It won't start. It won't go. It just makes silly noises and jumps up and down. TUBBY! WHERE ARE YOU?"

Tubby Bear didn't answer. He had heard Noddy's angry voice, and he wasn't going to say a word. He crept upstairs and hid under a bed. Tubby, what in the world have you done to Noddy's car? Oh yes—you cleaned it beautifully. But what ELSE did you do?

Noddy was so upset that he really didn't know *what* to do. Should he fetch Big-Ears? Oh dear, he had promised to call for him that morning and take him shopping! It was so difficult for Big-Ears to carry all his shopping home on his bicycle. Now he wouldn't be able to fetch him.

"Just wait till I get hold of Tubby Bear and find out what he's done to my car!" said Noddy to himself. "I'll clean it myself in future. Oh, my dear little car, whatever is the matter with you? Why do you keep saying Eekoff, Eekoff? What does it mean?"

"Ee-koff," said the little car, with a sudden little jerk. Noddy waited and waited for little Tubby Bear to come out into the garden, but he didn't come. Noddy had just made up his mind to go and fetch him, when he heard a very welcome sound.

It was the ringing of a bicycle bell!

"Big-Ears! Oh, Big-Ears, did you wonder why I didn't come and fetch you!" shouted Noddy, rushing out into the road. Yes—it was dear old Big-Ears, coming up to the gate on his bicycle, ringing his bell loudly to let Noddy know he was there.

"Noddy! Why didn't you come in your car and fetch me to take me shopping?" cried Big-Ears, jumping off his bicycle. "I waited and waited. Then I thought you must be ill, so I came to find out."

"Big-Ears, oh, Big-Ears, something dreadful has happened to my car," wailed Noddy. Big-Ears looked at the car in surprise.

"But it looks simply beautiful!" he said. "I haven't seen it so bright and clean for a long time. What's wrong with it?"

"Well, see what happens when I press the starter," said Noddy, and he pressed. At once the car said "Eekoff" very loudly, and jerked up and down. "Eekoff, eekoff, eekoff!"

"There!" said Noddy. "It keeps on and on

23

saying 'Eekoff' and jerking. It won't go. I think it's gone mad."

"Good gracious!" said Big-Ears, most astonished. "No—it hasn't gone mad, poor little car. It's got something *you* sometimes get, Noddy."

"What has it got?" asked Noddy, surprised.

"It's got *hiccups*!" said Big-Ears. "That's all. Listen—there it goes again 'eekoff—eekoff'. That's its way of hiccupping. And that's why it jumps and jerks—*you* jerk, don't you, when you've got bad hiccups!"

"Oh, *Big-Ears*! Has my little car *really* got hiccups?" said Noddy, very surprised. "It's never, never had them before. I didn't even *know* that cars could hiccup. WHY has it got them? How can I stop them? What am I to do? Why has . . ."

"Good gracious! Stop asking so many questions!" said Big-Ears. "Let me see now—people get hiccups because they've drunk something fizzy too quickly—or because they . . ."

"But my car doesn't eat or drink, Big-Ears!" cried Noddy. "You know it doesn't. It's ill! It's in pain! Oh, what shall I do?"

"It isn't ill. It isn't in pain. How can you be so silly, Noddy?" said Big-Ears, sounding quite stern. "What have you put into its petrol-tank? Did you put some different petrol—or have you poured something silly into it?"

"No—no, of course not!" said Noddy. "I only give it petrol. Oh, poor little car—there it goes, hiccupping again! Big-Ears, Big-Ears, tell me what to do! I can't bear it!"

"I think that little scamp of a Tubby has given the car something to drink—not petrol—some-thing else!" said Big-Ears. "It's upset it in some way. Go and fetch Tubby at once. Bring him here, if you have to drag him by the scruff of his neck!"

Big-Ears sounded so fierce that Noddy felt quite scared. He ran out of the garage, and shouted for Tubby. But there was no answer. Noddy came back, looking miserable. The car still said "eekoff, eekoff" and jerked up and down. What in the world could be done for it? Poor little car! It couldn't be driven. It couldn't stand still. It could only hiccup!

4. OH, YOU BAD LITTLE TUBBY BEAR!

"NODDY—we shall *have* to get Tubby here and ask him what he's done to the car," said Big-Ears. "He's done something—put something into the tank, perhaps, that's thoroughly upset the little car."

Noddy looked all round the small garage. There were tins in one corner, and a box in another. There was a shelf with little boxes of nails and screws and odds and ends. And there was another shelf with little stone bottles on it.

"Nothing much here," said Big-Ears. Noddy suddenly looked puzzled and went over to the shelf where the little stone bottles stood. "I don't remember these, Big-Ears," he said. "Oh —they're empty. What did they have in them?"

Big-Ears looked at them closely. "Ginger-beer!" he said. "GINGER-BEER! Noddy, have *you* been buying ginger-beer lately?"

"Good gracious, no," said Noddy. "I haven't

enough money for ginger-beer. Wherever did these bottles come from?"

"We'll soon find out!" said Big-Ears, and with Noddy following close behind, he marched out of the garage and went to the Tubby Bears' front gate. He swung it open, and went up to the front door. RAT-A-TAT-TAT! How loudly he knocked!

Mrs. Tubby Bear answered the door. "Oh, hallo, dear Big-Ears!" she said, pleased. "How nice to see you! What do you want?"

"I'd like a word with little Tubby Bear, please," said Big-Ears. "But perhaps you could tell me something before I see him, Mrs. Tubby Bear. Have you ordered any bottles of ginger-beer lately?"

"What an extraordinary question, Big-Ears!" said Mrs. Tubby Bear, astonished. "Yes—yes, I ordered quite a lot, because we all like ginger-beer, you know."

"Have you missed any bottles?" asked Big-Ears, in such a stern voice that Mrs. Tubby looked quite frightened.

"Er—well, yes, we did miss quite a few," she said. "We thought that our naughty little Tubby must have taken them to drink, you know. They—er—well—they disappeared rather quickly. I was cross because I was supposed to take the empty ones back to the shop."

"Well, there are a whole lot in Noddy's garage," said Big-Ears. "Quite empty. I want to see Tubby, please."

"Tubby! Tubby, where are you?" shouted Mrs. Tubby Bear. But no Tubby came. "I'll go and find him," said Big-Ears, firmly, and ran upstairs to Tubby's bedroom. There was no one to be seen, but Big-Ears' quick eyes caught sight of a small paw just sticking out from under the bed. He pounced on it and dragged out a very frightened little Tubby Bear.

"Ha! And may I ask why you are hiding?" said Big-Ears sternly, as Noddy and Mrs. Tubby came into the room.

"No, you mayn't," said Tubby, rudely. "Go away!"

He was slapped so hard by Mrs. Tubby that he

BIG-EARS CAUGHT SIGHT OF A PAW STICKING OUT

began to cry. "What did you do with that ginger-beer?" she said. "Surely you didn't drink it all?"

"No, I didn't," said Tubby. "I cleaned Noddy's car for him and he wouldn't let me put petrol in it and drive it—so I went and got the bottles of ginger-beer, and—and . . ."

"Tubby, you SURELY didn't pour the ginger-beer into my car's little petrol tank!" wailed Noddy.

"I did," said Tubby. "I thought it would go all right on that. It looked rather like petrol to me. But it *wouldn't* go. It—it . . ."

"Yes—we know what it did. It got hiccups," said Big-Ears, very sternly. "And it won't go. It just stands still, hiccupping and jerking. And it will take quite a time to get right, poor little car. Tubby Bear, what you want is a very, very good spanking!"

"I'll take him and give him one this very minute!" said Mrs. Tubby Bear, quite shocked to think of all that Tubby Bear had done. Tubby Bear gave a howl and disappeared under the bed again.

"I only gave the car a drink!" he wailed. "Its tank was almost empty. It was THIRSTY! It *told* me it was thirsty!"

"Rubbish!" said Big-Ears. "You wanted to drive it away for a treat after you'd cleaned it—but there wasn't any petrol—so you took your mother's ginger-beer instead, and poured it into the car's tank, hoping you could drive it on that. But you couldn't! All you've done is to spoil Noddy's little car! It will have to be cleaned out, and Noddy won't be able to have it till its tank is perfectly all right again!"

This long speech made Tubby cry even more loudly. He was hustled away by his mother, and told to undress and get into bed. "And there you'll stay until you say you're sorry, and empty your money-box to pay Noddy for any damage your ginger-beer has done to his car!" said Mrs. Tubby Bear. "I never in my life heard of such a thing—trying to drive a car on *ginger-beer*!"

"Will my car soon be all right again, Big-Ears?" said Noddy, feeling as if he wanted to howl too, like naughty little Tubby.

"Well—it will have to go for a good clean," said Big-Ears. "It looks to me as if Tubby has spilt ginger-beer all over your car's engine as well as emptying bottles into the tank. It will take some time to have it all cleaned. It will damage your car badly if you drive it now, all ginger-beery."

"But, Big-Ears—what shall I do if I haven't a car?" said Noddy, with tears in his eyes. "I can't take people about. I can't earn any money. What shall I DO?"

"Oh—we'll think of something!" said Big-Ears. "Cheer up, little Noddy. You've plenty of friends, you know. We'll think of *something* you can do. Don't worry! Don't worry!"

5. A WONDERFUL SURPRISE
FOR NODDY!

NODDY was very unhappy about his little car. It was now down at the garage being thoroughly cleaned and overhauled.

"The garage man says it will take at least three weeks before I can have it back," said Noddy, mournfully. "Oh, that horrid, nasty, unkind, silly, stupid, careless Tubby!"

"Dear me—what a lot of words you know," said Big-Ears. "Now just be patient, Noddy. I *think* I'll be able to get something rather exciting to use while your car is being mended. Just be PATIENT!"

So Noddy was very very patient, though whenever he saw his empty garage he felt very sad indeed. And then something very VERY exciting happened.

An aeroplane flew over his house, and then flew round and round, lower and lower—and landed right in Noddy's garden! Think of that!

An aeroplane landing in his garden! He just couldn't believe it!

Noddy ran into the garden, and the Tubby Bears ran out into their garden next door. An aeroplane! Landing in Noddy's garden! Whatever would happen next!

Well, will you believe it, who should jump out of the aeroplane but Big-Ears, followed by a very neat little airman. Noddy rushed to him.

"Big-Ears! What are you doing in an aeroplane? Where have you come from? Did you fly it—or did the pilot here fly it? Oh, Big-Ears, can I have a ride in it?"

"Now listen, Noddy," said Big-Ears, solemnly. "I have a very big surprise for you. Mr. and Mrs. Tubby Bear are so very sorry that little Tubby spoilt your car, that they have asked one of their cousins—this pilot here—to lend you his

aeroplane till your car is all right again. He will teach you how to fly it—it's quite easy —and then you can borrow it for your shopping and travelling till your own car is all right again."

"Big-Ears! I can't believe it! An aeroplane to ride in—one I can drive myself!" Noddy shouted at the top of his voice, he was so excited and pleased. "Let me get in! Oh, let me get in!"

"Well, you can *certainly* get in," said the jolly-looking pilot, who had been shaking hands with his cousins, the Tubby Bears. "But you mustn't fly it till I'm quite certain you know how to. It's very easy really."

"*I* want to get in. *I* want to fly it!" shouted little Tubby Bear in great excitement. He tried to push Noddy away. But Mr. Tubby Bear took hold of him and held him tightly under his arm. "Any trouble from you, little Tubby, and you'll go to bed for a week!" he said. "On no account are you even to get *into* the plane!"

He carried poor Tubby, kicking and struggling, into the house. Noddy couldn't help feeling sorry for Tubby, but he was so excited that he simply *couldn't* feel sorry for more than a few seconds.

An aeroplane for him to fly! Oh, what would everyone say? What would Tessie Bear say—and the Bumpy-Dog—and Miss Monkey—and everybody? It was the most exciting moment in Noddy's life!

"Get in," said the pilot. "I'll show you how to fly it. It's easier than driving a car. You don't have to bother about corners or going slow, or keeping to the left, or anything like that. You just fly it!"

Well, the pilot was right. It *was* easier to fly than to drive a car. Before twenty minutes had gone by, Noddy was flying that little aeroplane himself! Oh, what joy! Oh, what an excitement! Oh, surely he was dreaming all this!

No, you're not dreaming, Noddy! You are

flying a dear little aeroplane all by yourself, with Big-Ears and the pilot sitting close to you, to make sure you don't make a mistake and fall to the ground. But you're clever, little Noddy—even the pilot says he has never seen anyone learn to fly so quickly!

Now—down to the ground—see, Noddy, this is how you do it—gently, now, gently—watch that dial—it tells you how near or far to the ground you are—you don't need to keep leaning out. Gently, now—you're nearly there!

BUMP! That was rather too big a bump, Noddy, but, after all, it was your very first landing!

"Well done!" said Big-Ears and the pilot together. "Splendid, Noddy!"

"Oh, it was WONDERFUL!" cried Noddy, his face all smiles. "Is it really to be my aeroplane till my car's mended? Oh, what will everyone say? I'll fly over their roofs and shout down the chimneys—I'll fly round Mr. Plod's head and give him such a scare! I'll . . ."

"Oh well—if that's all you want to do with a very good aeroplane, I'll tell the pilot to take it away," said Big-Ears, in such a cross voice that Noddy felt quite alarmed.

"Oh, Big-Ears—I'm only joking!" said Noddy. "I'll be using the aeroplane to fly here, there and everywhere to do my shopping. I'll fly to the farm for milk. I'll give everyone lifts. I'll fly off and see all the people I know who live far away. Oh, WON'T they be astonished to see me landing neatly in their back gardens! I'll have to look out for the washing-lines, though, won't I?"

"You certainly will," said Big-Ears. "Now, for goodness' sake, get out, Noddy. I'm too fat for a small aeroplane like this. I feel quite cramped. Well, thank you very much, pilot. I think I can teach Noddy anything else he needs to know about flying. Really it's easier than driving a car, as you said to Noddy."

The pilot ran to catch a bus, and soon Big-Ears took Noddy up in the air again to show him quite a lot of different ways of flying—round and round—up and down—fast or slow.

"Let's loop the loop!" said Noddy, too thrilled for words. "I'll turn the aeroplane right over and we'll see everything upside-down."

"No, we will NOT," said Big-Ears, firmly. "I'm fat and heavy, and I don't want to find myself falling through the air and landing on somebody's chimney. Now let me help you to land in your own garden. It's rather a small place to land in, and we don't want to knock off your chimney. Now—gently does it!"

And, to the enormous astonishment of every one in Noddy's street, the aeroplane landed neatly in the very middle of Noddy's back garden! What a to-do there was! Mr. Plod came rushing up, shouting.

"Here, what's all this? Where did you get that aeroplane, Noddy? Who told you you could land here? How do you know how to fly it?"

"I'll take you for a fly, Mr. Plod!" cried Noddy. But Mr. Plod wouldn't go.

"You've no right to fly that aeroplane without a proper permit!" he said. "You come along to the police station with me, Noddy. We'll have to see about this aeroplane. Well, what next—you flying all over the town with Big-Ears! I never heard of such a thing in all my life!"

6. NODDY LEARNS TO FLY

NODDY and Big-Ears, followed by quite a number of people, and also by a very excited Bumpy-Dog, went along to the police-station. Mr. Plod listened to the sad story of Noddy's car being filled with ginger-beer by naughty little Tubby. Tubby, who was there, slipped off very quietly. He was afraid he might be well spanked by Mr. Plod!

"Now you listen to me, Mr. Plod!" said Big-Ears. "*I* got this aeroplane for Noddy. *I'm* paying for it to be lent to Noddy till his car's mended. So just be sensible and kind and give him permission to use it to take people about till his car's ready again."

"Yes. You tell him he can!" shouted everyone who was listening. "Hurrah for little Noddy!"

"Oh, very well," said Mr. Plod. "But the very first time you knock a chimney-pot off a roof, Noddy, or land where you shouldn't, I'll be after you, and lock up both you *and* your aeroplane!"

"You do sound cross, Mr. Plod," said Noddy. "Do come up in the aeroplane with us. You'll feel better then."

But Mr. Plod wouldn't, and Noddy and Big-Ears went out of the police-station. "He's a horrid old Grumpy," said Noddy. "And I've a good mind to knock his chimney right off his roof— bang, bang!"

"Now don't talk like that, Noddy, or I'll be sorry that I thought of getting you an aeroplane," said Big-Ears. "Go up in the plane again for half an hour with the instructor, and learn all you can. It's really not difficult."

"Oooh—I could fly it without a single lesson!" boasted Noddy.

"If you talk like that, you'll get swollen-headed and be too heavy for the aeroplane!" said Big-Ears. "Swollen heads are very heavy indeed. Now hurry up for your lesson."

Well, Noddy had two lessons and then he could fly the aeroplane just as well as he could drive his car. He wished very much that he had a hooter to scare off the birds that kept coming to see the aeroplane—and at last he flew

down to the ground, landed beautifully just by the garage where his car was being mended, and went to find his car. There it was, in a shed, half cleaned out already!

"Hallo—your car's not ready yet," said the garage-man in surprise. "Hey —don't take its hooter."

"I want it. I'm driving an aeroplane at the moment," said Noddy, proudly, "and the birds will keep getting in my way. So I thought I'd get my hooter. They'll hear that and get out of the way."

Off he went with his hooter, and fixed it into his aeroplane. Now the birds would be safe. Parp-parp! How surprised they were to hear a motor-hooter making such a noise in the sky!

Well, it wasn't very long before Noddy was just as clever at flying the aeroplane as Big-Ears and the instructor. "I think we'll fly down to the ground again now," said Big-Ears, "and drop the instructor. Then you can fly over the woods to my house, Noddy. Perhaps you'd better change places with me, and let me fly the

"THE BIRDS WILL HEAR MY HOOTER,"
SAID NODDY

43

plane now. There's a very nice hollyhock out in my garden—and my washing is there too, on the line—I don't want it spoilt—or the hollyhock knocked down."

So they dropped the instructor, and then Noddy and Big-Ears changed places. Big-Ears rose into the air once more, and flew over the woods. When he saw the roof of his toadstool house, he began to go down and down—and then landed with a bit of a bump on the grass just near his washing-line.

Noddy leapt out. He was so pleased with the aeroplane, and with flying, that he couldn't help dancing about all over the little garden, singing at the top of his voice!

"Oh, would you believe it, I've learnt to fly;
Up in the air I go, oh so high!
Maybe I'll visit the moon and the sun,
Or land on a star—oh, that *would* be fun!
I might find a rainbow, a-glittering bright,
And bring it back—what a wonderful sight!
Oh, would you believe it, I've learnt to fly;
Up in the air I go, oh so high!"

"Well, that's a fine little song about flying, Noddy," said Big-Ears, unpegging the clothes from his line. "Now I'll just go and get some ham from my larder while you lay my table for me. We'll have a nice little dinner and talk about what you're going to do with that fine little plane!"

They soon had their dinner and they talked and talked. Noddy talked the most—all about how he was going to fly over to Rocking-Horse Town, and ride the horses, and go to Bouncing Ball Town and catch some balls to bring home, and go off to Teddy Bear Town with little Tessie Bear, to visit her cousins, and . . .

"Stop, Noddy! You're making my ears ache!" said Big-Ears at last. "Where are you going to get the money to buy petrol for all these wonderful journeys?"

"Ooooh—I hadn't thought of that!" said Noddy. "Dear me, yes, I MUST earn some money, or I won't have anything to eat. Big-Ears, will people let me take them shop-  ping in my plane if I'm very careful with their parcels? I'm sure I could land neatly just by any shop they wanted."

"Well, we'll put up a notice in the post office about you and your aeroplane," said Big-Ears. "Now—do you think you can get your plane, and land it very carefully in the post-office yard? You'll have to mind the sacks of letters waiting there to be collected. And mind the post-office cat too—she'll be sitting near them."

Noddy was soon in his plane, with Big-Ears beside him. He flew slowly down into the post-office yard, feeling very excited. To think he could fly an aeroplane—and land it! *What* a dear little plane it was! Gently, Noddy, carefully now—mind that pile of sacks. That's right! Bumpety-bump. That was your wheels touching the ground. Now you're safely down!

So he was—and everyone came rushing out of the post office to see him and the little plane—postmen, dolls, teddy bears, a clockwork mouse, and a few Noah's Ark animals. How excited they all were!

7. TUBBY IS RATHER SILLY

"WELL, that's not a bad landing, Noddy," said Big-Ears. "A *bit* of a bump, but not much. Hey, everyone, get away! You can't get into the plane, there isn't room!"

Well, it was lucky that Mr. Plod came rushing up just then, or the little plane would have been swamped with excited people.

"Fly off!" he ordered. "All right, Big-Ears, you can get out if you want to. Noddy, go away. You can't park your aeroplane in the post-office yard."

While Big-Ears ran into the post office to put up a notice about Noddy doing everyone's shopping as usual, using his aeroplane instead of his car, Noddy pressed the switch that made the aeroplane rise into the air. But, oh dear, he didn't know that naughty little Tubby Bear was holding on to the end of one of the wings!

There he is, look, as frightened as can be, swinging by his hands, holding on to the end of the plane's wings. Everyone yelled to Noddy, "COME DOWN! COME DOWN! Tubby Bear's hanging on to the plane!"

But the plane's engine was making such a noise that Noddy couldn't hear. He flew off with poor little Tubby Bear clinging with all his might to the end of one of the wings, yelling and crying.

"Poor little Tubby—but really, it serves him right," said Big-Ears. "He spoilt Noddy's car, and what a little silly he was to catch hold of the plane just as it was going up!"

"Save Tubby, oh please save my little Tubby!" wept poor Mrs. Tubby Bear. "Ask that big crow over there to go up to the plane and tell Noddy that Tubby's hanging on."

Well, the crow was quite willing to warn Noddy and flew up into the air at once. But as soon as it

came near the plane, Noddy shouted, "Get away, crow! Can't you see my plane? It will fly into you. Go away!"

But the crow did its best to land on the plane, and Noddy used his hooter at once. "PARP-PARP-PARP!"

48

The crow had such a shock when it heard a motor hooter up in the sky that it flew away at once. Whatever next? Cars hooting in the sky! Really, Mr. Plod would have to do something  about it! The crow felt very worried indeed.

The little aeroplane didn't like Tubby Bear hanging on to it. It made it feel lop-sided. So it flew down low over the nice big pond in Mr. Golliwog's garden, and gave a jerk. Poor Tubby was thrown off, and down he went into the pond with a most terrific SPLASH! The aeroplane rose up into the air, and roared with its big voice.

"RRR-RRR-RRR-RRR!
Listen, you people down there, while I sing,
It's silly to hang on an aeroplane wing;
If you're REALLY wanting an aeroplane ride,
It's safer, much safer, to travel inside!
RRR-RRR-RRRRRRRR!"

Mr. Golliwog was sitting quietly reading by the pond, and the big splash made by Tubby soaked him from head to foot. He leapt up very crossly. "What do you mean, Tubby, by jumping out of an aeroplane into my pond and wetting me like this?" he roared—and poor little Tubby ran for his life! Oh dear, oh dear, whatever made him think that it would be fun to go up with an aeroplane?

"I never will again, never, never!" he wept, as he trotted home, a very wet and miserable little bear. "I'll never be naughty again, either. Nasty things happen when I'm naughty. Oh dear—I KNOW I'm going to be spanked for making my clothes all wet!"

Noddy was sorry for Tubby, but he couldn't help laughing. What a bear! What a little silly! Surely nobody but little Tubby would think of hanging on to an aeroplane!

"Well—he won't need a bath tonight, falling splash into the pond like that," thought Noddy.

He leaned out and saw Big-Ears signalling to him from the ground. He flew carefully down and landed with the very smallest bump just beside him.

"What made you fly off by yourself like that?" said Big-Ears, crossly. "You might have had an accident. And who was that falling

TUBBY WENT INTO THE POND WITH A
TERRIFIC SPLASH

into the pond? You surely didn't take anyone up with you?"

"Oh, don't be cross, dear Big-Ears!" said Noddy. "I *am* so enjoying myself! What shall I do next?"

"Well, I heard that Miss Monkey wants her luggage taken to the station," said Big-Ears. "She's afraid that if she waits for someone to give her and the luggage a lift, she will miss the train. So I told her to run to the station herself and leave her luggage in the back garden for you to pick up in your plane. Now can you land there, do you think—or shall I?"

"Big-Ears, I'm a very good pilot already!" said Noddy, proudly, and set off in the air again. He flew over Miss Monkey's house, and then went slowly down into the garden. It was a pity he landed right on top of

Miss Monkey's trunk, and dented it—but still, as Big-Ears said, there wasn't much damage—only a scratch or two. They put the luggage into the plane and off went Noddy to the station.

The train was in. Miss Monkey waved her umbrella madly at their plane. "Where's my trunk? The train's just going!"

Noddy was in such a flurry that he didn't think what he was doing. He gave the trunk a shove and it fell out of the plane at once. Down, down, down—BUMP! Where has it landed?

"Well—what a bit of luck! It's landed safely in the coal-wagon—on top of the coal, look!" said Big-Ears, with a chuckle. "The engine driver looked very surprised. I expect it made him jump, seeing a trunk come out of the air like that! You'll have to tell Miss Monkey that she owes you a shilling for delivering her trunk so cleverly!"

8. NODDY AND THE AEROPLANE

WELL, Noddy had a wonderful time that week delivering all kinds of things in his aeroplane, and carrying people to and from the station, or taking them to other towns.

It was all very exciting. He earned quite a lot of money too. But he did miss his little car. He didn't like to think of the empty garage at night. He wondered how the car was getting on. Was the tank clean yet? Was all the ginger-beer cleaned off? Would it go all right now—or would there be something so wrong with it that it wouldn't go properly any more?

Noddy kept going to the garage to ask about his car, but always the answer was the same. "Sorry—it's not right yet. Call again."

The aeroplane was great fun—but it wasn't like his own cosy little car that sang such a nice little song all the time. And then the aeroplane wasn't always very careful about landing —oh dear no!

Once it landed right in the very middle of Miss Harriet Kitten's roses, and Noddy had to pay her for each broken bush. And another time, when he landed, one of its wheels knocked off Bert Monkey's hat, and it rolled into the pond. He was very cross.

"Why don't you tell that plane to look where it's going!" said Bert, angrily. "Now I can't wear my hat, and the wind's cold, and I'll get earache. Well—if I have to call the doctor, *you'll* have to pay the bill. Unless you like to take me up in your plane for a ride?"

"No, I wouldn't," said Noddy. "I don't trust that silly tail of yours! It would come creeping round my arm and try to steer the aeroplane— then down we'd go, CRASH! I think I *won't* take you for a ride, Bert Monkey!"

Then a dreadful thing happened. Noddy was just dropping slowly down to the road to land Mr. Noah by the Ark, when someone came rushing by on a bicycle. Noddy didn't see him coming, and, oh dear, the person was

knocked off his bicycle, and his hat rolled away into the gutter.

Noddy landed and leapt out of the plane to help. Oh dear, oh dear, oh dear—it was Mr. Plod he had bumped into! His bicycle lay in the road beside him, and his helmet was bowling merrily down the street.

"I'm sorry, I'm sorry, I'm sorry!" said Noddy, his head nodding madly. "I didn't mean it. I didn't, did I, Mr. Noah? Oh dear, Mr. Plod's so angry."

Yes—he certainly was. He hustled poor Mr. Noah into the Ark, and then he called to Noddy.

"What do you mean by that dangerous bit of flying? You did it on purpose! You saw me on my bicycle, and you knocked me off. Fetch my helmet at once before it rolls miles away. And you can hand that aeroplane back to its owner, or else I'll put you into prison. I never heard of such a thing in all my life—knocking people down, bicycle and all—and just look at my helmet, rolling into that puddle. Just you wait, Noddy—JUST YOU WAIT!"

But Noddy didn't wait, he was so very frightened. He ran off as fast as he could to Big-

Ears' Toadstool House. He left the aeroplane behind. He'd never fly it again! Oh dear, WHY did it have to fly down on Mr. Plod? Didn't it like him? Oh, wasn't Big-Ears at home? Noddy did so want him. He was trying not to cry now. Oh, would he be taken to prison for hurting Mr. Plod? Oh—oh—OH!

The last OH was a very big, sad one. Big-Ears wasn't at home! Where was he, then? "BIG-EARS!" shouted Noddy. "I'M IN TROUBLE! I WANT YOU, DEAR BIG-EARS!"

He sat down at last to listen for Big-Ears' bicycle bell. He must have gone shopping. Well, he'd soon be back. "I'll listen for the tinkle-tinkle of his bell," thought Noddy, and listened so hard that he almost fell asleep.

And suddenly he heard a noise that made him leap to his feet. It wasn't the tinkle of a bicycle bell. No—it wasn't that. It was —yes, it really WAS a noise that sounded like "PARP-PARP-PARP!"

"It's my *car*! I know it is! It's my own little car. Oh, it is, it is!" cried Noddy, and ran down the path.

And there, coming up to the Toadstool House, was Big-Ears—and HE WAS DRIVING NODDY'S CAR!

Noddy ran to meet him, and the car was so pleased and excited that it jigged up and down and said "parpparpparp" without stopping. Noddy leapt into it, and put his hands on the steering wheel. He sang a very loud song indeed.

"Oh, here's my little car again,
　　Hallo, little car!
　　You're feeling very well, it's plain,
　　How full of joy you are!
　　You're jigging up and down for me,
　　Parp-parping as you go,
　　I feel as happy as a king,
　　Dear little car, hallo!"

Big-Ears stood beside him, laughing. When Noddy had finished, he clapped him on the back.

"A very nice little song, Noddy!" he said. "I *thought* you'd sing for joy when I brought back your car."

"How did you get it, Big-Ears, dear Big-Ears?" cried Noddy.

"Did you hear how I knocked Mr. Plod off his bicycle? Oh, you should have seen his helmet bowling down the street into a puddle, you really should!"

"I heard all about it," said Big-Ears. "I rode up on my bicycle and was most surprised to see your aeroplane all by itself with nobody in it—and Mr. Plod raging round, holding his muddy helmet in his hand. He said he was going to get hold of your car and keep it so that you never had it again, as a punishment for you."

"Oh, how DREADFUL!" said poor Noddy, looking really scared.

"Don't worry, I took the hooter to the garage and found the car was ready to go back to you. So I paid the bill and brought it up to the Toadstool House myself for you. And there it is—and there you are, in it! What about singing a very nice little song about me, as a payment for all I've done?"

"Oh, I will, I will!" cried Noddy, jigging up and down in his little car. "Oh, you are wonderful, Big-Ears, the best friend in all the world! Oh, I do love my little car; and oh, I'm SO happy! Listen to my song, Big-Ears; it's for you, all for you!"

And Noddy sang this song. Big-Ears liked it the best of all Noddy's songs, and I'm not surprised, are you?

> "Oh, dear old Big-Ears,
> I do love you so!
> You're my very good friend,
> The best that I know!
> I love your white whiskers,
> I love your red hat,
> I love your big smile,
> And I do love your cat!
> I love you to visit me,
> Trundling along
> On your old bicycle,
> Singing your song.
> Oh, DEAR old Big-Ears,
> I *DO* love you so!
> You're my very good friend,
> The best that I know!"

LOOK FOR THE NEXT NODDY BOOK